12-15-15

ALL ABOUT ME
Briana's Neighborhood

Dream Big

Readers are
Leaders!

Best,

S

Written by Sahar Simmons
Illustrated by Nicolette Morgan

Heidi Mann, Final Touch Proofreading & Editing, LLC
http://FinalTouchProofreadingAndEditing.com

Printed and bound in China by Aomeiya Printing Co. Ltd.
www.aomeiya-printing.com

ISBN 978-0-9838 492-0-9

For more Briana info and to order books go to
info@brianasneighborhood.com
www.brianasneighborhood.com

IT'S ME BRIANA, LLC

Briana's Neighborhood

This book is dedicated to my little brother Sterling.

This is the groundwork for you to achieve anything that your heart desires.

Dream big, little brother!

Love you, Sahar

About the Author

Sahar Simmons was born and raised in Brooklyn, NY. Briana's Neighborhood is her first published book series. Sahar's childhood experiences are the inspiration for Briana. Sahar is a graduate of Hampton University and currently resides in Atlanta, GA.

About the Illustrator

Nicolette Morgan is a freelance illustrator who resides in Atlanta, GA. Briana's Neighborhood is her first published work. Nicolette is currently working with her father on a children's book.

I don't want to move! Moving means that I'm going to have to leave my favorite bloc

and all my friends and favorite places. My mom is the Assistant Principal at Centra

High School and just got a new job as Principal at Carver High School. I'm really happ

for her because she is so excited, but I'm sad that we are moving to a different par

of Brooklyn. Mom says I'm going to love the new block and my new room. I really don'

want a new block or a new room.

My name is Briana, and I'm eight years old and in the third grade. I want to tell yo

about myself, if that's okay. I'm from New York City, also called the "Big Apple." I d

not know why it's called the "Big Apple" because I don't see any apple trees growin

in my neighborhood. But it doesn't matter because I have lived in Brooklyn my whol

life and I love New York.

I'm an only child, and I live with my mom, Debra, and my grandma, Pearl. I call my grandma "Nana" because I did not know how to say "Grandma" when I was a little girl. Nana moved to New York when I was only three years old, when my daddy moved to California.

I live in a very tall building that stands all by itself on my block. I like to ride up and down in the elevator with Mom and Nana. It's fun because you never know what floor it will stop on or what neighbors you will see. I like to stop at the sixth floor because that is where Ms. Ross lives. She has the cutest dog, and I love to pet him. Sometimes Mr. Jacobs rides the elevator, but he is a little grumpy and doesn't talk that much.

Right across the street from my building is a playground. My friends and I love to play all kinds of games. We play hopscotch, tag, and jump-rope. We don't have a lot of grass in my neighborhood, so we have to be careful not to get hurt. My mom call it "city living," and she worries that I don't have a lot of places to run and play. She grew up in Atlanta, Georgia, and had a lot of space when she was a little girl.

In my neighborhood, we have Mr. Henry's Ice Cream Shop and Tony's Pizza. Tony's Pizza has the best pizza in the world! I don't think I can live anywhere else. I bet Mom didn't have stuff like this.

In the summertime, it's so much fun when all of the neighbors get together to have one big block party. There is so much food, music, and tons of great games to play. When it gets really hot outside, the fire hydrant is turned on and we all run around and splash in the water.

Our neighborhood park has big hills. In the wintertime, we make snowmen and slide down the hills. My mom says they didn't have any snow in Atlanta. No snow? I don't know how she had fun in the wintertime. I really have a great time in Brooklyn, and especially on my block.

When I'm not playing outside with my friends, I like to pretend in my favorite place. I love my bedroom and the yellow color on the walls. I pretend that I'm Oprah Winfrey, the famous talk-show lady on TV. I love to talk to my dolls and stuffed animals. Mom and Nana let me pretend in front of them, too. My mom says that sometimes I talk too much, but Nana loves it when I talk about everything.

I like to draw pictures of the sun, snow, and rain, and I try to guess what the day will be like when I wake up in the morning. I pretend I'm the weather lady on TV. Some days, when it's raining and cold outside, I want to have a sick day like my teacher sometimes does. My mom just laughs and says it doesn't count for kids. I don't know why, because everybody gets sick sometimes.

Every day after school, Nana picks me up and we walk home together. We only live three blocks away, so it's not too far for Nana. Today I am feeling sad about the new house. My new house will be too far for us to walk to from my school. How are Nana and I going to have our walks and talks? Nana loves to walk because she says that exercise is very important. She says that's why she stays so healthy. I think Nana is going to miss our block, too. Ms. Appleton is her very best friend, and they trade recipes all the time. Nana just tells me not to worry.

I love spending time with Nana when my mom has to work late. Sometimes we just sit outside in the park and she tells me stories. I tell Nana that I'm really going to miss my block. It's going to be hard making new friends. What if nobody likes me? "Briana, sometimes we can't see the big pot of gold that's waiting for us on the other side of the rainbow," Nana says. "You may not see it now, but change is good. Don't you worry because Nana and Mom will be right by your side." I am really happy I have Nana around. I know my mom is happy, too.

On Saturday morning, Mom takes Nana and me to see our new house. It's a very prett

block with rows of brick houses and lots of tall trees. Wow! We don't have this man

trees on our old block. We are moving into a house that has three floors, and two o

them are just for us! Ms. Huckleberry is our neighbor who lives on the first floor, an

guess what? She has the cutest little puppy, and she says I can walk him anytime

want!

Our house is much bigger than our apartment. Nana's bedroom is on the main floor s

she doesn't have to walk up the stairs all the time. My bedroom is so pretty. I have

huge window and lots of room for my dolls and stuffed animals. Mom says that I ca

also paint this room my favorite color, yellow.

Mom says she has a surprise for me. We walk outside to the back of the house, and I see the prettiest backyard with flowers and a tree with a swing. "Ms. Huckleberry says that the little girl who used to live here loved this swing," says Mom. "I thought it would be perfect for you!" My very own swing and backyard! I have never had that before. I think I am going to really like my new house.